The Sparrow and the Tortoise

By Randal Gilmore
Illustrated by Chung-Hui Ho

This book belongs to:

_____

_____

_____

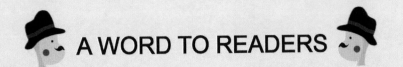# A WORD TO READERS

The Sparrow and the Tortoise is the thoughtful tale of a sparrow's journey to discover what is real and what is just a reflection. The journey begins near a pond of crystal clear water at the base of Mt. Fuji in Japan. The Mirror Pond, a National Natural Treasure of Japan, imagines this backdrop. An exploration of The Mirror Pond online is worth the effort; how much more an actual visit in person. Other parts of the story also take their inspiration from people and things you may recognize. Matsuo Bashō truly is one of Japan's most famous poets from years gone by. The Giant Buddha, located in Kamakura, Japan, does indeed stand hollow and absent of any life. Windows in its back open to the outside for tourists to look out. Meanwhile, giant sandals, never worn, hang on a nearby wall. The words quoted by the young man as he prays in the courtyard originate from Psalm 115:5-7 (ESV). The steps of Mt. Fuji are stops at various intervals on the way up the mountain. The words sung by the old man at the top are lyrics from "I Will Lift My Eyes" by Jason David Ingram and Jeffrey Stephen Norman, used by permission, as per the copyright notice on the title page. Finally, it's worth remembering that sparrows really do sometimes struggle with the meaning of life and a sense of self-worth. Still they sing joyfully to their Creator, ever listening to Jesus' reassuring words from Matthew 10:29-31a; "Are not two sparrows sold for a penny? And not one of them will fall to the ground apart from your Father. But even the hairs of your head are all numbered. Fear not, therefore...."

A sparrow flew over a forest, searching for water to drink.

But not just for any water. The sparrow thirsted for water from the Mirror Pond at the base of Mt. Fuji in Japan.

The sparrow looked down in time to see the pond's crystal clear water and a young girl sitting nearby.

The sparrow landed next to the water and
leaned forward to take a refreshing drink.
Then the young girl said:

Looking exactly like
Blue flag iris: blue flag iris
Inside the water's shadow

The sparrow stood up straight with its eyes opened wide.

"I did not mean to frighten you, little Sparrow. Those were the words of Matsuo Bashō, a famous poet from the 17th century. He once saw a blue flag iris reflecting in water like this and wondered, 'Is everything just a reflection?'"

"When I saw your reflection, I could have said:

    Looking exactly like
    Sparrow: sparrow
    Inside the water's shadow

    "Am I just a reflection?" the sparrow thought,
as it slowly flew away.

Sometime later, the sparrow returned to the pond, hoping to see the young girl again. But, alas, she was nowhere to be found.

"It's sad to be just a reflection," the sparrow thought. For even sparrows know that reflections have no life or beauty of their own.

Just then the sparrow noticed a tortoise stepping its way from the other side of the pond. "Ohayou," said the tortoise, "what brings you here?"

The sparrow told the tortoise what the young girl said about its reflection in the water.

"I see that your heart is troubled, my little Friend. You will find help, if you fly to the Giant Buddha."

"How wonderful to be called the friend of someone so wise!" the sparrow thought.

Soaring high into the air, the sparrow flew in the direction of the Giant Buddha.

Soon the sparrow landed in the courtyard in front of the Giant Buddha and stood gazing into its face. But nothing happened.

Then the sparrow noticed a young man standing a short distance away next to a pair of giant sandals hung on a wall. The young man bowed his head, as if to pray. When he looked up, the young man saw the sparrow tilting its head to one side.

"Hmmm," the young man said, "you think I was praying to the Giant Buddha. I was praying, but not to the Giant Buddha. I was praying to the Living God. Think on this, my little Friend:

They have mouths, but do not speak;
Eyes, but do not see.
They have ears, but do not hear;
Noses, but do not smell.
They have hands, but do not feel;
Feet, but do not walk;
And they do not make a sound in their throat.

"If you look behind the Giant Buddha, you will understand."

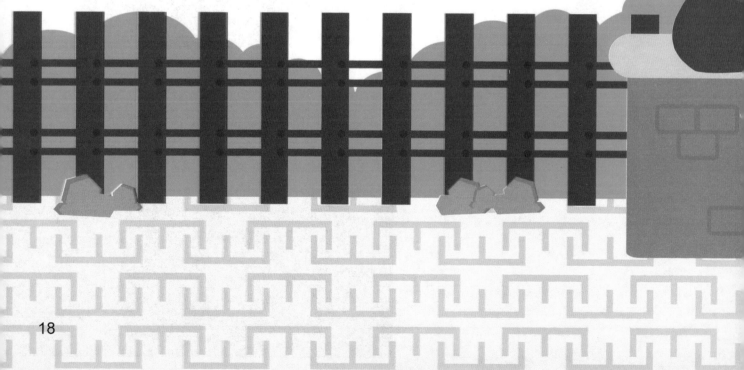

"Living God? Behind the Giant Buddha?" The sparrow dashed to the back of the Giant Buddha, where it discovered two large windows. The sparrow fluttered in and out of both windows again and again, but saw nothing.

The sparrow returned to the pond and found the tortoise sunning itself near the same spot as before.

"How was your journey?" said the tortoise.

"I am more confused than ever. What do you know about the Living God?"

"Ah, yes, the Living God. Sooner or later, everyone who visits the Giant Buddha wonders why it is hollow and lifeless."

The sparrow waited for the tortoise to say more, but the tortoise only closed its eyes and sat in silence.

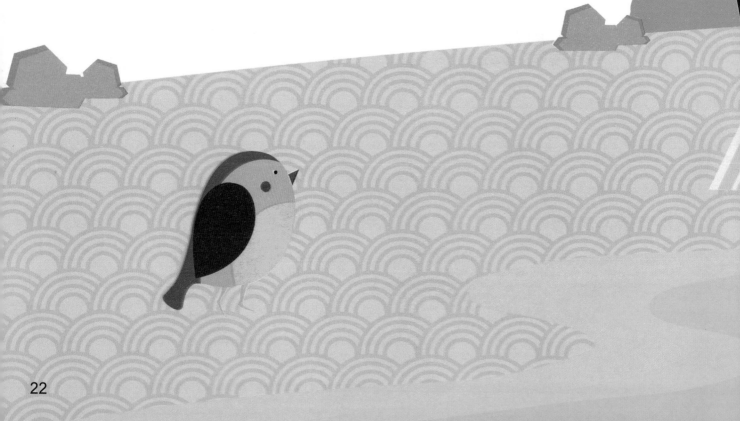

Finally, the tortoise spoke again, "Now you must fly to Mt. Fuji, my little Friend."

"Is that where I will find the Living God?"

"Fly to Mt. Fuji," said the tortoise. "You will see."

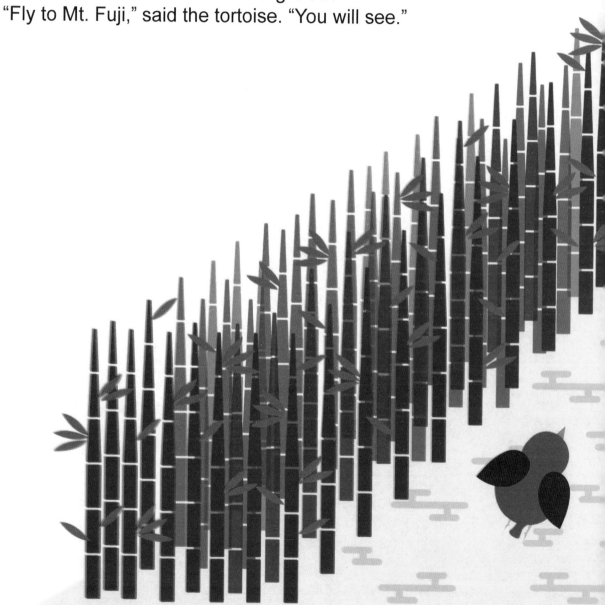

The sparrow hurried to Mt. Fuji, wondering why the tortoise seemed so confident.

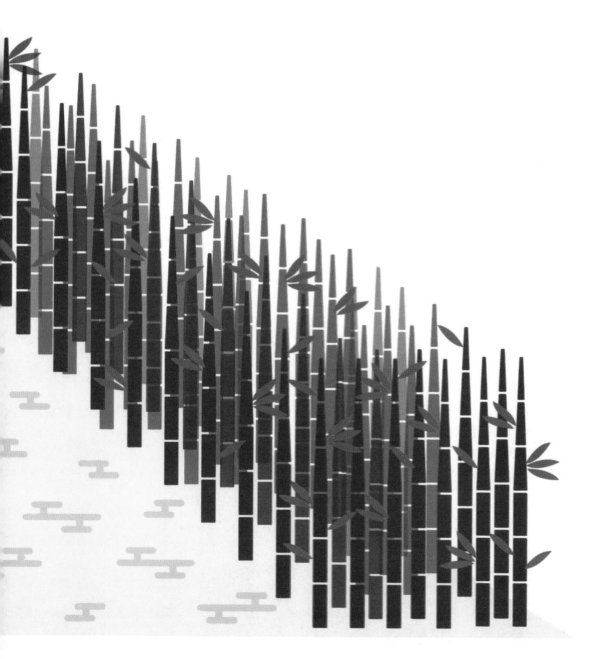

Higher and higher, the sparrow flew, until it arrived at the tenth step, near Mt. Fuji's peak. The sparrow turned its head this way, then that way, looking for the Living God. But again there was nothing.

"I cannot go on," the sparrow thought.

Soon another visitor arrived at the tenth step, an old man who had started up the mountain early that morning. The old man lifted his head and looked into the sky to catch his breath.

Then he began to sing, with his hands raised to the clouds. The sparrow flew closer to listen to the beautiful melody and words:

I will lift my eyes to the Maker
Of the mountains I can't climb
I will lift my eyes to the Calmer
Of the oceans raging wild
I will lift my eyes to the Healer
Of the hurt I hold inside.
I will lift my eyes, lift my eyes, to You.

"The hurt I hold inside? These are words I can understand," the sparrow thought.

The old man lowered his arms and started to walk down the mountain. The sparrow took flight to follow him, longing to hear more. But a stiff wind kicked up from the opposite direction, knocking the sparrow back to the ground. By the time the sparrow recovered, the old man was gone.

The sparrow flew back to the pond to meet the tortoise once again, trusting that the tortoise would know what to do next.

"Who is the Maker of the mountains?" said the sparrow. "And who is the Living God? I need your wisdom to understand."

"You do need wisdom," said the tortoise, "but not the wisdom that comes from me. You need the wisdom that comes from the beginning."

"The beginning?"

"Yes," said the tortoise, "in the beginning, the Maker of the heavens and the earth created everything, including you and me and the mountains we can't climb. The Maker is the Living God. He does not live in temples made by human hands, nor is He an image, like the Giant Buddha. And no one can imagine what He looks like. Still, the Maker is a good and wise King. He created you. He put his life and beauty in you. It's what makes you so much more than just a reflection."

The sparrow and the tortoise stood together quietly, as the words of the tortoise went deep into the sparrow's heart.

"I am unworthy of this honor," said the sparrow, as it bowed its head, unfolded its wings to the heavens, and flew away.

One day the young girl returned to sit by the Mirror Pond as before. Soon she could hear the distant sound of a carefree heart singing, "I will lift my eyes to the Maker...." The joyful sound grew closer and closer, until the shadow of a familiar sparrow flew across the surface of the crystal clear water.